Dani's Tale

By Hayzel Greene

Written Summer 2013 and Fall 2017

Copyright 2017 Hayzel Greene for Aisha Taylor

Published by Hayzel Greene Publishing

Cleveland, OH 44106 USA

Cover Design: Mogul focus

Edited by: Aisha Taylor & Thomas Smalls

ISBN: 978-0-9965936-1-8

Printed in the United States of America

Dedication

October 28, 1970 – March 13, 1995

This book is dedicated to Ms. Taleetha Reni Sharon. Your smile will continue to live on within my heart. Our times together were priceless. You will always live within me. Rest in Peace!

Acknowledgments

To my Taylor Made Family and Fisher Clan which I am a product of and my lineage runs deep.

To my family, friends and associates; I am shouting out to all you who had / has faith in my abilities. You know who you are!

To my ride or dies: Jeannie, Ty, and Raquiyyah here I go again.

~Hayzel

Preface

There is a plan that is written. You are a witness as to how it unfolds. The people that cross your path and the incidents that mold your existence is just a fraction of the story called life. My name is Dani and I am a female child born to a man who has many sides. Studying his calculated moves taught me life lessons. Not to say that I got everything correct the first go around, but I think I did well for myself. I must say that my journey was an interesting one. I have gone through many trials which I think I landed on my feet. Although things could have gotten a little bit hairy if you know what I mean. Doing too much as I may say.

I am in love with Al and Al is in love with me. Not for sure if we are a fairy tale romance, but I am sure we are kind of interesting. Without trying to spoil the inside pages, I can say that although the same incidents occur to people they can and will view it differently with some similarities.

All secrets do not come to light. But at the end of the day, do they hurt you or make you stronger? Well, hell…spoiler alert. I love Al. Al loves me. Wes fucks me and I fuck him. Wes is stuck and I am too. Candy is not as sweet. At least not to me. Daddy is a boss and I am his understudy. Stace is left out and she is none the wiser.

I think I did that right? Beyond this page, you will meet me, Al and Wes, along with a few other characters that will mold a time span of a few years in our lives.

Hope you enjoy!

Dani

Dani

As I said before, my name is Dani and I have a story to tell as we all do. Mine is short and brief but interesting at the same time. I have encountered people that have molded who I am today. I guess this is the part when I lie on the couch and tell my life story without boring you or taking up too much of your time. Short, sweet, but to the point.

Dani

In my thirteenth year is when I finally realized that my dad was a Mister. I guess there are worse things that he could be. I knew girls in school whose dads were cocaine and heroin addicts. Walking around stealing and doing shit to get that next high. I guess I was spared. I could have had a mother who turned out to be a crackhead. Living an unstable life. Daddy had money. He didn't splurge; he spent and invested wisely. I thought for a long time that our lifestyle was gravy since he owned The Gentlemen's Club. The premier nightclub/bar in the hood. Everyone knew that was the place to be. Even had teen nights for me and my friends. Talk about an amazing dad. Mine was awesome.

Outside of the club, he owned other property. So, as far as I was concerned, having a few hoes wasn't a bad thing. All this together explained why we had the best of things. Come to think of it, I can't say that I ever wanted for nothing. I do, however, have to check myself, before I start claiming shit, saying I had it going on. The reality of the matter was he had it going on and I just reaped the benefits. How about that?

Early on, my dad had girlfriends, a lot of girlfriends. Shit, in my eyes, I thought he was the man. He was handsome with a nice build. Why wouldn't women flock? Regardless of all the women, he loved my mother and my mother loved him. She was first. But the truth of the matter, his status dictated what the deal really was.

Now, don't get me wrong, I didn't care for all his women. I have questioned my mother often in the attempt to find out first, if she knew about these women, and secondly, why was it okay? Most of them were cool and cordial. I gravitated to some more than others. Stace became my favorite. Over time they became my friends, my confidants and in some perspective, my role models. Even still, there were times I acted a little stank and had to check myself. I figured out that they showed no ill will towards me. Did nothing but show me love in their own way.

Children could be cruel. Whenever the bullies in school wanted to go in on me, they would say shit like "yo stepmom's a hoe." I didn't think that was the most creative thing that could have been said. The thing is, and I was taught, most bullies have issues. So, they try to take their hurt out on someone else. On some occasions, I was that person. Which didn't make me a bit of difference. I had tough skin. My dad taught me, and I learned very well. I constantly stayed in fights. Never was suspended because the principal was friends with my dad. God doesn't like ugly, and he ain't too fond of their stupid asses either. If only they truly knew the dirt I had on most of them anyway. Our town was not that big, and folks talk. Especially the ladies who frequent The Gentlemen's Club. My dad didn't hold too many secrets from me either, and I was not sheltered from the day to day activities in the club. It was nothing for me to sit in the dressing room or at the bar sipping a ginger ale where I can hear all the gossip. So, I would laugh when the mean kids came after me because I knew all the secrets that were supposed to be kept about these children's fathers. Shit, mothers too! Being as ignorant as I am, after laughing and warning them to get out of my face, I would let them have it and spill all the tea. "Why your clothes wrinkled today? Oh yeah, you couldn't iron because your dad couldn't pay the light bill because his ass was at the club making it rain," I said with the snap of my fingers, then walked away. I think this made me more of a target. But I didn't give a fuck.

From the outside looking in, my life was cake. Nice clothes, nice cars, nice jewelry, just overall good shit. I didn't want for anything. As long as my grades were good, and my chores were done, I was smooth sailing. But with every teenage girl, there are moments where things could be grueling. His so call protection and lessons learned made me a bitch. I guess he meant well, not wanting me to be blind to the facts, turning out to be anything like the women who lived at the club.

My mother passed away when I was five. So, I was a daddy's girl. For years, it was just him and I. I was not Daddy's only child. He had a basketball team with some on the bench. He wasn't funny-actin'; if the women had other children, he claimed them, too. At least, I think, he had ten biological children in total, with me being the youngest. The only ones that I've met were those who came by from time to time with their hands out. The others, well, I guess they figured the money that he sent to their mothers was good enough.

When his girlfriends started coming to the house, it was a welcome to have another female around. My daddy taught me the basics of being a young lady growing to womanhood. He held nothing back. I am sure that my friend's conversations with their parents about their periods were unlike mine. A lot of times I must laugh to think about how we had that talk. He sat me down and cut straight to the chase.

"You are on your period, which means you can get pregnant. You will bleed at least once a month, so make sure you stock up on your pads. If you start fucking around, make sure you have that nigga wrap it up. You don't need any babies right now. Most importantly, make sure you clean yourself more often than usual because period blood can stink. And you don't want people talking about you. That is a no no." He got up and that was it. Left me sitting there with my mouth wide open.

There were a few things he left out. Like how to use a tampon. I guess it there is a good thing that I had Stace for that. In some ways, she was a lifesaver. She was there to pick up the pieces that Daddy dropped. She taught me how to truly cook, clean, and how to woo a man.

Most of the others confirmed it, but Stace was the true mother figure. Daddy had a rein on his women. So they knew not to step out of line when it came to me. One of the things that was interesting was, my dad, well he liked to test them out prior to putting them out there. So, while most kids learned Sex Ed at school, I learned at home. Shit, I learned how to become a woman. My dad taught me the hustle, but the game raised me. I was given the game through his eyes. A girl child born to an alpha male.

When I was seventeen, I graduated from high school. My present was a lifelong lesson; don't let a man run game on you, you run it. Although I paid very close attention to my surroundings and how my dad did things, I was still a little hesitant about moving out of my comfort zone. I was popular in school by now: head of the yearbook committee, captain of the debate team, junior student council president, and a few more. I knew what the rewards were by doing good in school, so I was about mine. Didn't have time to court or be courted by a boy; shit, for that matter, I had never been kissed.

By the age of eighteen, I was unsure if I was on course or not. Things began to change. I realized that I was crushing on someone. It was kind of weird because I never paid attention to him like that. Plans change, and shit happens, right? Especially when I truly recognized Alford. All it took was one dream. He always wanted us to call him Big Al because he said Alford sounded nerdy. Whatever! I guess it's strange for me to come into these newfound feelings. He was always around. He was Stace's nephew. He was here every summer like clockwork. He was my playmate for close to five years. I would say we were close. Ask him and he will tell you the same. Over time, we learned each other. We grew together and at some point, I fell in love and I believe the feelings are mutual.

Can't actually say when the feelings started to develop, maybe if I hit rewind I would have a better idea. Regardless, when it happened, I know that the summer of his eighteenth year, he noticeably changed. For that matter, we both changed. His voice got deeper, and his body began to develop: arm muscles and a six-pack. Me, I got breasts and my ass popped. He was always nice-looking, but for some reason this summer, he was breathtaking. I had to check myself. This man who stood in front of me couldn't have been my Al that was just here last year. Damn, what 365-days can do! Our unspoken relationship was finally established. He was my first hug, my first kiss, my first everything. We shared a lot. I don't believe we had any secrets. And this summer we would share our bodies. And with that, I would no longer be a virgin.

Our first time will be calculated. We must not get caught. Most just let it happen. Me, well, I knew I wanted Al and I am for sure he wanted me. We were used to Daddy being gone at a certain time. So, we knew exactly the day and time, I would submit myself. It wasn't uncommon for Al to bring up the sun at my house. We slept in separate beds so there was no need for anyone to think suspiciously. Friday night would be the day. Daddy, Stace, and the rest of the girls went to the club. It was time to take it to another level. That I would use what I learned to show him that I've grown into my womanly skin. No more Lil Dani. That night we will graduate from Sorry and Monopoly to Chess and Backgammon.

I was hesitant, but I was ready. At least I thought I was. We stood watching each other as we peeled our layers. Either we were moving in slow motion or we had a lot of damn clothes on. I stood there with my bra and panties on while he took off his boxer briefs. Now what came next, I think I wanted to close my eyes for. Oh wait, I can't, this is happening to me. I saw it pointing right at me. My first thought was, "What the hell is he going to do with all of that?" Then my realization was he's going to give it to me. I took off the rest of my covering and stood baby-born naked. He extended his hand, pulled me closer, and we began to slow dance. Not until then did I realize that the radio was on playing "Anniversary" by Tony Toni Tone. I caught a chill, not the cold kind, but a flash of goosebumps. He laid his hands on my shoulder and kissed my neck. I became less tense and began to accept his advances, which turned me on even more than I already was. We kissed before, but for some reason, these kisses were unlike the others. I found myself sucking on his tongue. I was on fire, and he was my personal civil servant equipped with his own hose. We have listened to the Quiet Storm in the past, but tonight they were playing all the right songs. I broke our bond and I climbed on the bed and waited for him to join me.

I closed my eyes and pictured an episode watched within my dad's closet when I was stuck after rambling hoping not to get caught for being someplace I had no business. He brought someone in the room before I could escape. It was either hiding under the bed or run into the closet. The closet was my choice. So, I sat on the floor while they had sex and I was forced to watch. Well, I wasn't forced; I could have closed my eyes. I did for a minute, but I will tell you one thing, just the thought of my dad getting his groove on was a little gross. So, I lay on the floor and put my earbuds in until I fell asleep. When I woke he was gone and those images were burnt into my brain.

Damn! Clear your mind, clear your mind. I was back. Al! The moisture of his lips on my breast opened the door for his passion.

Now the strange thing is he didn't climb in between my legs as I thought he would. Instead, he put a pillow on the floor and pulled me to the end of the bed. Resting the back of my knees on his shoulders, he began to lick my pussy. He opened me up and sucked on my clit and rubbed my pussy's mouth. I thought I was going to lose it. His touch was soft.

The slight heat of his breath was soothing. Chill bumps overpowered me again as I lay and let him have me. He began to speak inaudibly as I lay with my eyes closed gripping his head. "What?" I said. Not for sure if I really wanted to know what he was saying, or if I wanted him to finish talking and shut up, so he could continue. At that point, we made a pact that we would be together forever, no matter what. As I got wetter by the second, he entered his finger. He pushed it in and out as I received him. I lifted to meet him and rolled my hips. My body, at that point, had a mind of its own. As he sucked harder I began pulling away from his suction. Crawling towards the top of the bed, he pulled me in closer sucking harder. Not for sure how long he was down there, I felt an indescribable sensation starting from my toes. It scared the shit out of me at first. What the fuck? I started having convulsions. I covered my mouth, trying to keep my screams to myself. He reached up and grabbed my arm, pulling my hand so that he could hear my cries. Shortly after, I felt an intense calm followed by heavy breathing. He coaxed me into grasping the feeling, enjoying my moment. I jerked around like a fish out of water. Breathing heavily, I managed to call his name a couple times, which I believe hyped him. He was all in it. Damn, is there a tutorial on eating puss? He mastered it.

"Cum for me," he said.

He stuck two fingers in making a come-hither motion and rubbed my clit real fast with his thumb and sucking my overflow. That shit felt so good that I grabbed my own damn head.

Shortly after, I said, "I cumming".

"Well, come on then." He said as he spits on my clit and rubbed faster.

I did just that. I came. I started to move because I thought he wanted to get up. Little did I know that he wasn't finished. He continued to eat as I lay exhausted from my feat. Pulling myself towards the top of the bed, he climbed in between my legs. He grabbed a towel next to him and wiped his face.

"Damn girl, you sure had a lot to give," he said. "How long has that been pinned up in you?"

On his knees, he stroked his dick rotating around his head. He was anticipating what was next. His dick began to expand; growing outward, I wondered when it was going to stop. I asked myself repeatedly, in my head, am I ready for this.

In mid-thought, he attempted to enter me where my body resisted. He was too big. "Hold up! Shit, wait," I cried out, letting him know it hurt.

"Sorry." With the help of some lube, he rocked back and forward slowly piercing me, opening me up little by little until he was in enough for his liking. I flinched in pain. Clinching the sheets and then his back, I am sure I left broken skin.

"Fuck."

"My fault, but that shit hurts." He lifted from on top of me. I wonder if he is mad. He went down and began licking me again. Wetting me, he climbed back up and began rocking until he was in. I felt him dig into me more until I felt his resistance. "What's wrong?"

"Nothing, I got this." He said with a little grunt. He continued as he whispered into my ear "I love you." I was open for him, pain and all. Tears streamed from my eyes as he kissed my eyes and licked away my tears.

He must have known something that I didn't. "Are you ready?" he asked in a whisper.

Ready for what? I thought. "I guess," I answered calmly.

He pushed one time and I felt a pop, tensing my body in pain; I cringed.

"Damn, you alright?" he said, pressing and breathing heavy into my ear

"No, but it is what it is," I said with tears in my voice.

"I love you," he said proudly.

"I love you too." I exchanged

How the fuck did my dad leave that shit out? I might have reconsidered if I knew all this pain was involved. "Well, that shit hurt like hell," I said frustrated. "I hope it was good for you because it wasn't good for me."

I asked myself over and over, why didn't I know that it would hurt like it did? Shit, I was new to this, but guess who wasn't? This nigga right here. He was no stranger to the task. I guess this was a secret that I was not privy to. This tid bid of info would have been important.

He kept apologizing for his part in my pain and promised that it will feel better the next time. I reluctantly smiled. He continued his motions switching spaces until I felt the same calming feeling earlier. My fear and pain subsided, and I became excited. He took a few more strokes and we came together. Wet, I stuck my hand in between my legs drawing back blood coated fingers. "Why am I bleeding?"

"It is official, you are no longer a virgin, and we should celebrate," he said excitedly.

Why the fuck his ass so excited? This wasn't a fuckin' vacation. Pleasure, pain, and then pleasure. This is some bullshit. But I was a big girl. I decided to give myself to him as a woman, so I had to stand in it and act as the woman I was or was becoming. We got up and showered. I sorely stood in the shower, crying, feeling the pain that resonated between my thighs. He grabbed me, hugged me, as most things we did together, he joined me and cried. I got out of the shower, I got dressed, and I immediately lay down because not only was my mind exhausted, my body was tired.

Summer went on as usual. No recognizable changes. We went to the movies, the park, and of course to the club. There was no way in the world that I would tell my dad or even hint on to the fact that I gave up my womanhood. The season was dwindling as it always does. However, for some reason, when we parted this time I believed it to be a little different. Not for sure why I felt this way. I just did. He called me every morning to make sure I was awoken for school, and then at night to find out how my day was. There were times where he would call during the day just to check on me. I loved this about him and that was the good thing about our relationship. There was always something to talk about. The phone calls were nice, but face to face was so much better to me. Especially now, since we took our relationship to another level.

He called me daily for about two months. Then the calls dwindled to 3 to 2 times a week. I chalked it to school. Oh yeah, he was accepted into an HBCU down south. Of course, he called when he got his acceptance letter. Not to mention Stace couldn't wait to tell the other ladies that Al was accepted. Of course, I was proud. Me, on the other hand, I stayed at home. I think Daddy is slowing down. Some days he didn't seem like his old vibrant self anymore. I guess you can call it an occupational hazard. I decided to stay home and enroll at Cuyahoga Community College. This way I could continue my education and keep eye on him. Al had a full course load, so our times on the phone were not as long as they use to be. I guess I just chalked it up to higher learning. Later, we were down to what appeared to be every other week. It was truly strange, and I felt that something was wrong, but hey, at least I have my summers. Time to find something to occupy my time as much as it hurt, I should understand that shit changes. At least I have my memories. We did promise ourselves to each other no matter what.

The schoolhouse wasn't the only place I learned how to maneuver. I was a quick study. I watched Daddy for many years, but paid attention as I got older. Now, since Daddy is spending more time at the club and less out on the block, it was time for me to step in and put a new spin on some thangs. I studied him, the girls, the tricks, and the money. Throwing a little Accounting 101 and Economics 201 in the pot, this recipe was for nothing but success. I thought I was ready. So, I put my money where my mouth was. I started my transition by just holding conversations with the ladies; I didn't want things to get awkward. Don't get me wrong, I was not trying to take over. Call it an expansion. Knowing my dad, I had to come correct. So, I made sure I had everything down pat. I set up a business meeting with him. I sat down with Daddy in an official capacity. I had to let him know my interest in the business with me running men. Something small, a few nice-looking men that fit my criteria. He was open to the idea. But I had to prove myself.

My business plan outlined the perspectives, key players, capital, and financials for three years with major profits. Daddy enjoyed a good read, especially one that spells out money. He gave me the green light and at that moment I was born. My Daddy was Mister and I was Mademoiselle, Daddy's Girl. We were a team, an unstoppable duo, as we were when I was five. Excited, I went to The Gentlemen's Club to begin my scouting. Tonight, was gentleman's night. Top shelf was half off. No doubt it would be some fine ass brothers there. I walked in dressed to the nines with my fuck em pumps on. I stepped to a few pitching and spitting game.

I had impromptu interviews just to see if I wanted to put more time and effort into them. Some were game off rip, and others thought I was bullshitting. So, me, with a little gift of gab, spit some pimp shit letting them know how profitable it would be for them. That we are all squirrels out here trying to get a nut and we need to get in where we fit in. Shit, who they think they are fooling? They come up in here trying to see who they can choose and then go fuck sumin'. So why not get paid for it? Oh yeah, and I guess the fact that I was frontin' new clothes were the lick. I think that's what sealed the deal for some. Done deal! Niggahs live to be sagged out and blinged up. Some concerns were raised as to what services they would have to offer. I assured them that not all rendezvous resulted in a fuck or a suck.

My men were a little different than the women Daddy employed. I didn't tolerate standing on the corner. There was no need to stand on the stroll. It wasn't like they needed to pick up any random bitch. Every customer came through me. I then assigned them the way I saw fit. Depending on what the client needed, which gentlemen she would have.

My first client was Sandy. She was about my age. She wanted a date to a family reunion. She was tired of her family badgering her about not being married or having a steady man in her life. I met up with her to get a run down on her history. This way her date would know just enough info to pull it off. Not to mention I need to ensure my assets. No need for no crazy bitch to be clockin'. She needs to know what is expected of her and what she was getting from my men. All clients were not just for fucking, some just wanted company. I could care less, especially if the money was good on the wood. Cash and credit only. No checks accepted. I met at her house to complete the transaction.

I went back to my office, which was my bedroom for now, until I can clean out my junk room. I looked at all my profiles and matched her with Wes. I thought he was the ideal date based on what she was looking for. He was clean cut; attractive, 22, 6'2", 250lbs of solid muscle, chocolate, with a nice taper fade. I took him shopping so that he could literally dress the part. One thing that is important you must show that you are a woman of your word. It is funny when I met Wes, I thought he was the corniest. His pickup lines needed work.

As I sat there and watched him try on several outfits made me look at him in a different light. He started to look fine, not a trick-ass niggah out for hire. Now, when I met him, he caught my eye, but I was on a mission. So, I had to stay focused. Not to mention I was committed. But damn, the way he looks now makes me wonder why I didn't keep that for myself. I think I had to catch myself on several occasions dazing out or focusing too hard on that body ody. Damn his dick print gave me a welcome distraction. I had to laugh at myself because just recently I was scared of the dick, running away from all that Al had to give. Since I am what you say a 'Newbie' and Al promised me that it wouldn't hurt the next time. I thought about it very hard. Maybe I'll let Wes follow up from the rear.

He looked good in Polo. The tailored look fit that ass just right. For some reason, I had to stop myself from staring. But he wasn't stupid by far, he caught me a few times and with that, I think he decided to play along. How, you may ask? Well, he came out with only his drawers on asking if I could hand him another shirt. When I tell you his six-pack damn near looked like a bonus eight, I had to adjust myself a little. So, I had no problem going to get him another shirt. I needed the distraction. After we left Ralph Lauren we went to Macy's to find a couple tailored suits. Like a kid in a candy store, he was delighted as to what my money could buy him. Unbelievably, he had a little swag about himself and spending this little time with him gave me a new outlook than the one I had when I saw him sitting at the bar. Sandy was pleased and assured me if she had another function that she would keep me in mind.

Being a Daddy's girl, I had to sample him. After all, he belonged to me anyway. At least I think that is how it works. Yeah, that's how it works. My game, my rules. It couldn't be awkward. I had to know what I want and go get it. This was a decision I had to make on my own. I couldn't ask for advice. So, I was a G about mine. I told him that I thought he was sexy as fuck, and that I wanted some dick. I think I caught him off guard. But he was game. We met at the tellie off I90 in the next town.

He got there before I did. I guess he was excited. The room was booked and prepaid. I stopped at the desk to retrieve my key and headed upstairs. The room was nice, king size bed with a Jacuzzi tub.

To clear the awkwardness, we discuss his duties to the women he took out on the town. It appeared as soon as we finished our impromptu meeting he began to undress. He truly had no shame in his game. He did not waste any time; luckily, I took a shower before I got on the road. I think my clothes hit the floor in a matter of seconds. No real foreplay, just straight to it, he began by licking my lips from bottom to top. And I don't mean the lips on my face. He stopped at my clit a couple times, sucking and tugging. He most definitely was no stranger to eating pussy. He smacked on each lip teething uncontrollably. Sticking his finger in, he finger-fucked me, adding finger after finger until he comfortably added three. I couldn't take anymore. I was on fire. The thought that he had more to give had my mind blown. I couldn't wait until he fucked me. It had been two-months since I laid in Al's arms. Man, I miss him. What the fuck? Why am I thinking about him right now when I got this nice-ass-looking hunk of a man's head between my legs carrying on a conversation that only he knows what he is talking about. My mind went blank and my toes curled as my orgasm traveled up to my mind to my cooch where I cried in ecstasy. I remember this. I came, and he licked and sucked all my juices as they flowed from within. If I didn't know any better, I think he bought his "A" game. Shit, is this something I want to share? His dates might have to be sexless.

He climbed on top of me. Stopping on his knees, he inserted his dick into a Lifestyle or a Magnum, by the time I peeped the pack was thrown. Safe sex! I like that. Kissing me on my neck and then my nipples as he wanted to make sure I was hot and ready before he positioned himself to give me him. Licking his fingers, he rubbed his hand on me; spreading my lips, he rubbed his head on my clit. Sensitive from my last encounter, I jumped. I parted for him to enter. The bell was big; his head disappeared, opening me to make way for the rest of his long, thick dick. He fucked me long and hard. I came two more times. Damn, he was good. Not to say this is crazy, but he wasn't finished. He asked for me to turn over on my knees. I did. I heard the tear of another pack and the snap of rubber letting me know that he was switching out. All I could think of was Oh Shit, is this nigga going to try to fuck me in the ass? I don't think I can take that. So, I braced myself. I held my breath tensing up not wanting to experience this for real, but I was so hot and horny I couldn't begin to form my lips to say no. If there was such a word at that time. He began to stick it in and I flinched, making that sound that truly doesn't have a spelling to it. He apologized and stuck it in the right hole. It didn't take him long to pick up his rhythm. We were back to it.

I can tell that he was finally ready to bust him one. He wrapped his arms around my waist and laid on my back as if we were one. He smooth R&B rhythm became sixteen of the damndest bars a rapper could ever spit. When he pulled out, he made the loudest moan/scream combination that I have ever heard.

I say our outing was successful. The ladies loved them some Wes, which was fine. But he wasn't the only one I had. So, I introduced the other gentlemen to their roles. Unlike Daddy, I was good with fucking Wes, I didn't need to test the other ones, besides, I'm not a hoe I don't need that many dicks up in me. I made Wes my Bottom Bitch. He was on my arm (not literaly). I couldn't let Stace see that. As the days went by I started to think less and less about Al. My first love was leaving me. Wes had my heart now. He nurtured me, took care of me when I was sick, went to work, and bought me all the money. He was the ideal man. Now I started feeling some type of way, it started becoming difficult to share him with other women even if it was for dating and conversational purposes only.

"Daddy, I think I am in love with Wes!" I said one day during our Sunday dinner.

"What about Al?" he inquired

"Daddy, I haven't heard from him in a minute. I am getting used to being with Wes."

"Baby Girl, I have to confess. Remember when I switch phone companies? Al tried to get in touch with you on your old phone. I told him that you went to a convention out of the city and that as soon as you got your new number you would be calling him. He said that he will be here this summer to see you as usual."

"Daddy, why would you do that?"

"Because I was trying to make sure your head was in the game. Couldn't let your love for him cloud your judgment. I needed you to bring your 'A' game".

"Daddy, I can't believe you!" I shouted as I got up from the table. "How the hell am I going to explain Wes to Al? Had I known, I would be better prepared."

"Dani, if your game is good, you wouldn't have to. Wes will fall into line. He will give you your space because your man will be home for a couple months. He will then take his place when Al leaves, Baby Girl. That is a part of the game," he said sternly.

"Daddy, for your sake, I hope so!" I said as I walked out of the dining room.

Although Wes had his own place, he stayed at my house nightly. He made sure I woke up to him next to me. Now that Al is coming to visit, it was time for him to go home. Al couldn't know that he was sharing my bed, that we couldn't sleep together when he was in town. Our roles would have to go back to me being the head and him bringing up the rear, so to speak. That business is what it is. I would continue to send him out on dates as I do the others. He hesitantly agreed.

The day came, and Al was in town. I was overly excited to see my man. I sat in the car outside of baggage claim. Until I knew he would be there. I stood anxiously waiting, as soon as I saw him, ran to get a hug and a kiss. I truly longed for his touch and smell. The majority of the conversation was catching up. It was nice to be in his presence. We had planned to get something to eat after we dropped his bags off. I didn't let on that he was having a surprise party waiting for him.

I let him go in first, as soon as he walked in everyone yelled a combination of welcome home and congratulations. He was surprised and gave me one of the biggest hugs and kisses of thanks. I was surveying the room looking for Wes when I saw him near the staircase with a sour-ass look on his face. When he saw that I caught his looks he tried his damndest to control his facial expressions. I read him, and he was not a happy camper.

Everyone was mingling and enjoying themselves. Al and I stopped and talked with several people. My text alert went off and I excused myself from the conversation to read what it said: "This some bullshit! I don't know what the big deal is? But I am out of here. Can I see you upstairs for a minute before I bounce? Come to your Dad's office." I returned to Al's side to excuse myself from everyone for a business matter.

I went upstairs to Daddy's office. As soon as I walked in the room, Wes closed and locked the door. Pushing me down on the couch, he lifted my skirt, pulled my panties over and proceeded to suck on me with aggression. As my mind told me to stop him, my force field was lacking. My arms became limp. I had no control as he bit my clit. Sucking and fingering me simultaneously, it took me no time to bust. Before I could gather myself, he arrested me. Throwing me over the couch, he assaulted my pussy with his huge humongous dick raw dog. This nigga is crazy. What if we got caught. He fucked the shit out of me. I guess the thought of Al being downstairs fueled his passion. How could I explain that shit? Well, it is done. He came hard, burying his face in my back to muffle his scream of ecstasy. We came together. As I fixed my clothes I told him that we couldn't do this anymore. As I said that, my mind sang another tune. I think this was the best fuck I had had in a very long time. I took a hoe bath and fixed my clothes before I returned to the party. I reiterated that we couldn't do this while Al was in town. He hesitantly agreed if I promised that when Al went home he would allowed back in my bed. I did.

If the thought of Al brought this out, I think I will make that a regular in our bedroom conversations. I thought Al would have a problem with me expanding Daddy's business. He said he did not. I was glad. The rest of the summer was wonderful. I had the opportunity to lay with my man. Enjoying him for the summer as I did every year. His presence, his conversation, and his bed. Summer ended. Al returned to school. Wes was back home. Business as usual. Like my Daddy, I got hoes.

Al

I guess it is my turn. My name is Al. I was once Dani's boyfriend, but now I am her man. My life leading up to her was truly interesting and I wouldn't change it for the world. However, I will give it all up if it meant that I could spend the rest of my life with her. The thing is, what you don't know all the time will not hurt you. Once you know, you have to decide what you want to do with it.

Al

They never understood why there is where I wanted to be. Every year like clockwork, I waited for that last bell to ring in for summer back. I was on my way, bags packed a week ago. I was going to see her. I would prefer more time, but if this is all I was given I was going to take it. We developed a bond that was different from the rest. So, I choose every year to be with her. To spend time! To get to know her! To one day let her know that I knew her not so-secret-secret. For years I bounced from relative to relative until I finally realized that although we look alike, there is something just a tab bit different between them and my aunt Stace. The more time I spent with her the more I realized that she was just a little bit more to me than my aunt. No one would tell it, but I knew. Forgiveness is a powerful thing, and some take it with a grain of salt, but love overpowers a lot. Mine was strong and one day I will tell her that I do forgive her for giving me up. That I understood, that because she was a hoe in the literal sense of the word, she did what she thought was best for me.

Stace worked at The Gentleman's Club. Some nights were better than others, and most times she was whipped. So, I knew to have a hot bath ran, candles lit, and her favorite Taylor Made Scentsations wax burning. When she took off her makeup and that lace front she was more beautiful than the mask that she wore. I guess she wanted to be someone else. For a while, I just couldn't understand how someone who looked like her, and talked as she did, needed to be what she was. Standing 6'2", her stride commanded attention. If you switched her wardrobe you would swear she was a corporate girl. People do what they do to make them happy or to get by, but it is not for me to judge.

Coming more often Stace surprised me for my 14th birthday a bedroom all my own. I had no problem sleeping on the pullout sofa. This apartment was so much nicer than the one she lived in on the Westside. Walking in everyone yelled "Surprise"! Most of her friends from the club came. I was used to being around them. Even Candy! Candy was my first. I would never tell Stace, but Candy really tasted like Candy. Like a Jolly Rancher, I think it was Strawberry.

One-day last year Stace was called to attend a private party. It was our weekend together and she felt bad that she had to go. I understood. Money talks and bullshit walks. I was too young to be alone, so she called a friend over to "babysit" for a few hours or the night whichever was sooner. She hurried and dressed, looking flawless as ever.

"Have a good time," I said.

"Will do." She returned as she kissed me on my forehead.

Candy was my babysitter. I've seen her before. She came by and chilled with Stace on occasion. I never hung around to listen to the latest because one thing that I did learn is, when grown folk talk, children should excuse themselves. I went to my room to get prepared for bed. I stripped, wrapping my towel around my waist so that I can take my shower. I didn't notice at first that Candy was in the doorway watching. She smiled as I tucked my wrap. I guess she liked what she saw. It was low key weird because I was only thirteen and she had to be at least five years older. After my shower, I returned to my bedroom to dress in my usual shorts and T-shirt. As my ritual, I turn on the radio to listen to the latest jams as I drift away. Candy must have felt some type of way in the living room alone. As soon I settled and began to shut my eyes, she summoned me. Never was I prepped to see Ms. Candy legs gapped on the couch, naked as a jaybird. Don't ask me what that means because I have never seen a jaybird naked, but I have heard that saying before. I hesitated. I don't know if at that moment I was afraid or excited. Shit, a little bit of both, because I felt a little different than when I walked into the room. My dick started to grow before me.

She watched as I stepped slowly inching towards her. My first mind said retreat into my safe haven, but that one tiny piece of my brain or the devil on my shoulder said to go and see what she wanted. She said she had a secret to share with me and only me. I bit! Watching, she coaxed me to come over. I approached slowly. Shit was playing in slow motion. The apartment wasn't that big, so in all actuality, it didn't take me long to get there. When I arrived, she grabbed my hand and put it on her breast. Pulled me to my knees collared me and forced her tongue into my mouth. It was cold and clammy. I tasted garlic. I see this on TV. I got this. So, I started moving my tongue right along with her.

I think I was in a groove because she took my other hand and moved it between her legs where I felt thin razor stubble hair and moisture. My eyes popped like a deer in headlights. This is where my lesson began. She instructed me to kiss her nipples one at a time. She told me to circle my tongue around them as if I was licking my lips. I did as I was told. She threw her leg on the back of the couch, handed me a long thick rubbery thing that reminded me of myself. Not for sure who my dad was but he truly passed me down his loin. She said to stick it in slowly. I did! She moaned and moved her body like a snake. I moved down closer to get a view of this thing going in and out. I occasionally looked up to see what she was doing. This is the first time that I was close enough to a pussy to see what it felt and smelt like. She wanted me to find her bud by opening her lips more. Of course, I found it, it wasn't hard. Well, it is not like it was really hiding. It was just neatly tucked away. She instructed me to lick it. I was kind of hesitant. "Lick it?" I said to myself.

"Lick it." She said again.

I lifted my head some to figure out how to lick this little bud thing as she called it and continue to push this rubber in and out. I situated myself and could do both. She moaned louder than before. I pulled back to continue watching and she said to keep licking. I did! I began to suck harder as I became uncomfortable in my shorts. I began to feel restricted. Fixing myself, I lifted and dove in. Losing myself sucking and licking while I thought of ways to push and pull her toy in and outside of her. She grabbed my head and pushed my head down with intensity. She tasted like her name. So, I had no problem at this point to continue this secret of ours. Thinking of the Tootsie Roll commercial. How many licks does it take to get to the center of this pop? She started shaking and her legs tensed. I didn't know what was wrong, she startled me. After a while, she calmed. She said she wanted me.

She summoned me on top of her. With her legs still gapped, thighs wet from the pleasure I climb on top of her and replaced me. I did the same thing with my dick as I did with her toy. She was warm. She was wet. She called out my name. Told me to go faster and harder. In my mind, I thought I was doing the damn thang. I guess not, so now I have closed my eyes and thought about the DVD that I watched over Ralph's house.

I slowed my pace and let the feeling take over me. Every time I pulled out I felt a cool breeze not only up my spine but on my dick. I can't tell you how many times I pumped but shortly after I felt the urge to release something. I closed my eyes tightly and bit my bottom lip. She moaned for me to keep going. But I couldn't. I hoped she would not be mad. What does she expect? This shit feels good. I think I am going to have to do this again. I felt light, good, and drained all at the same time. I smiled to myself as I felt my squirt.

I was done. Stick a fork in me. I pulled away from her and sat on the couch with my eyes closed. My breathing was a little off. But I was trying to catch up to it. She started me when I felt the warmth of her mouth on my dick. I jumped. Now by this time I shriveled up. But she kept sucking until I grew in her mouth. She sucked on me bringing into reality my own porn. Reflecting I grabbed her head and pushed it down, allowing her to put all of me into her. Excited, I CAME again. I tried to rest as I was truly tired. I have no clue what time it was.

Hearing Stace's car door closed, we jumped. I grabbed my shorts and ran to the bathroom. Wiping her pussy juice off me, I walked out the bathroom catching my footing and rubbing my eyes as if I just woke up to go to the bathroom. I couldn't believe what just happened! I got in the bed. Stace didn't know and I didn't tell. Every chance we had, Candy would add to my sex resume.

~~~~~

Every summer was loads of fun for us. This year Stace introduced me to her friend Dave. I often heard her talk to him on the phone. But he was just a voice until I met him face to face. I shook his hand like I was the man of the house. I guess rightfully so, I was the man in Stace's house. At least that is what I told myself. The cool part of hanging out with Dave was that he had a daughter. She was beautiful and smart. So, she was added to my summer. We hung out on the days/nights Stace had to work. She introduced me to her world. Just as I anticipated seeing Stace every summer I looked forward to seeing her as well. When we were not together we talked and texted. But every summer like clockwork we were each other's rock. We shared almost no secrets. At some point, not for sure when, maybe it was two summers out. I fell in love. I had Dani in my mind and heart and had Candy in my bed.

As the years past, I changed. I grew into my manly form. My voice began to match my Adam's apple and my dick got bigger. Even though I didn't need it. But adding a couple inches throughout the years made me more desirable to the ladies. Trust me, women are dick watching. Dani and I never talked about sex between the two of us. I think it was sort of implied that we would be each other's first based on her conversation and my avoidance of the real question. So as time went on we planned our...oneness? Is that what it is? Shit, that sounds corny. I believe. Let's keep this shit 100. I was ready to hide the sausage or put the needle in the haystack. Nah, I think we were planning our oneness, the beginning of our physical to mesh with our mental and emotional. Hey, fuck around I'll be writing my own greeting cards. But seriously, I gave Candy my body, but I wanted to give Dani my world. I knew I was her first hug and her first kiss. Now I just wanted to be her first everything.

Stace and Dave went out for the evening. Instead of going home to Stace's I decided to stay with Dani. I was sure Candy would be just a little salty because I knew she was longing for some of me. But she'd get over it. At least I thought she was until she kept blowing me up. I mean damn, how many times do I have to send your ass to voicemail before you see that I am not answering. I think after what appeared to be 50/11 times, she stopped. Damn! Can we say get a life other than mine?

We talked about taking our relationship to the next level. I didn't want to rush her, but my appetite to experience her was starving. She agreed that we will share our bodies with one another. As we began to undress we made a pact that this will be the beginning of the rest of our lives together. That we will forever belong to one another! Undressing her I remember seeing her in a different light. I figured since my first time found my face in Candy's lap Dani would enjoy it as well. Laying her on her back, I pulled her close to the edge of the bed resting her knees on my shoulders. I began to lick and suck until she called my name with convulsions. She was cumming, I talked her into grasping the feeling, relaxing and embracing the feeling as I sucked all her sweet juices. She didn't taste like Candy, but she had something that I know I would be craving for a long time coming.

"Are you ready?" I asked softly.

"Yeah," she answered slowly catching her breath

The look on her face didn't go along with her words. I wanted to stop and talk her through what happens next, but when I tell you I was sooooo ready. I became a little selfish. It was all about me feeling the inside of her. I so wanted to melt. I positioned her legs so I would fit. I began to slowly pierce her. She flinched and clinched all at the same time. Now I knew that I had to talk her off the ledge.

"Relax and breathe," I said tenderly.

"I'm trying. Just make sure you don't hurt me." She said.

"Never will that be the reason."

After she appeared calm, I started to insert myself again and she ripped into my flesh. Shit, that stung. I pulled back and grabbed the bag of condoms and lube I bought from the store earlier that day. I went back down and kissed her lips and licked her until she became moist again. I put some lube in my hands and rubbed her mouth hoping it was enough for me to somewhat slide in. Little by little I pushed my way in. She held on for dear life. And I let her. My heart was beating fast. My torn flesh was secondary now to how she felt. Boy, this was truly something different from Candy. Actually, this felt better. The struggle to fit is real! The more and more I disappeared within her, she pushed me back bracing herself. As I reached the back, I felt some resistance. I knew I was not all the way in. Pushing harder I saw a tear roll. I kissed her eye and licked away her pain. Hoping that she was ready I reared back and gently pushed with force when I felt a pop.

"Damn, you alright?" I said, pressing and breathing heavy into her ear

"No, but it is what it is." She said with tears in her voice.

"I love you," I said proudly.

"I love you too." She exchanged

Now that I popped that. It was time to make her feel like I know I could make her. Something smooth as your favorite R&B song. I glanced at her and saw that her face still displayed frustration. "Baby, what's wrong?" I asked, although I already knew the answer to my question.

Frustrated, she said "That shit hurt like hell. I hope it was good for you because it wasn't good for me."

"Baby, I am sorry you are hurt! I will make it up to you, I promise. The next time it will be awesome."

She allowed me to finish. I kissed her soft, juicy lips passionately to show her where my mind was. It was all about her at this point. I had to score some brownie points so this either wasn't my last time or it wouldn't be forever for my next opportunity to make love to my Love. I slowed my pace to assure I wouldn't come without her getting hers. I had to make sure that she felt pleasure to top the pain that I caused her.

When it was over she rolled over in a fetal position and laid. I kissed her back and her shoulders. I apologized multiple times for her being uncomfortable. I grabbed her hands helped her into the bathroom. I joined her in the shower and we cried. If I thought I was in love before I was truly head over heels now.

~~~~~

It was the inevitable. My departure. The summer was coming to an end. I think I started missing her prior to my departure. I spent as much time with her as possible. Candy kept blowing my phone up. I couldn't understand why she couldn't understand that Dani was my girl and she was just a fuck. I guess that meant nothing because she started to get jealous. Threatened to let Dani know what the deal was between her and me. Of course, I had to let her know if she overstepped her bounds and did some grimy shit like that, she wouldn't get none of this dick anymore. I guess she changed her mind.

When I got home it was business as usual. Having graduated from school, I had to get a job. Working took a toll on me. I was forever tired. The money was good, but I began to slack on contact. Showing my family that I was responsible and able to make my own money I was allowed to accept my entrance into Drake University. I had to call Dani to catch up and let her know what was going on with me. Since we committed ourselves mind, body, and soul, I had to stay on task as much as possible. But with the absenteeism, our relationship began to change.

Dani decided to stay home and go to school. I wished that we would have gone to school together and got an apartment. Started our life together as husband and wife. It will just be a matter of time; I know our love will one day give us that opportunity to play house until she is ready to tie the knot. As fate would have it, Dave became ill and her staying home was warranted. She began to take over the ongoings within The Gentleman's Club. I was so proud of her. She even expanded by adding men. Stace kept me informed, especially when her phone broke. One day I was going to be able to buy her her own club. We will name it is The Ladies Lounge.

I worked hard this school year and watched the clock on the last day before summer break to anticipate being held by wifey. I feel almost as I was anticipating my visits with Stace some five years ago. I made sure I had a straight flight. No delay to get to mine. When I made it downstairs to baggage she stood with a sign that said, "Welcome Home Baby!". I grabbed her first, swung her around, kissed her passionately before I put her back to her feet. She followed me to get my bag.

We reached Dave's house in a matter of minutes or at least it seemed. I walked into a surprise party for me. I was just that, surprised. Everyone was there. Stace, Dave, a couple of the other ladies and even Candy. Wow! I thought I left her at school. There were a couple guys there that I was not familiar with. Walking me around the room I was introduced to a couple gentlemen. Folks were extra chatty. It was cool, I was the man of the hour. Dani's phone started going off. She looked down. Put it on vibrate and apologized. It continued to pop off. I told her to go ahead and take it seeing as though it may be business. She excused herself and walked off. I looked around and all the usual suspects were present at least I thought they were. I was bombarded with questions. I laughed and caught everyone up on college and dorm life.

It seemed like she was gone for a while. I hope everything is okay. I decided to go and look for her. I excused myself from the chatter. I went into the kitchen and she wasn't there. I headed upstairs to see if she was in her dad's office. As soon as I hit the top stairs, Candy asked if she could talk to me for a minute. I told her that

"I'm busy right now. I will talk to you later." I said aggravated

"It will not take that long. Just give me a few seconds of your time. Please." She pleaded.

"I'm looking for Dani, have you seen her?"

"No, I wasn't looking."

"We had this conversation already. I told you now don't start tripping. Why are you here anyway?" I said as I grabbed her arm and pulled her into the guest bedroom to continue this conversation. I could already see her making me go off. She needed to go. She was going to get sloppy.

"Look, I love you," she said.

"Okay, why are you telling me this now? Today is not the time for all of this. Dani is somewhere in this house and you are trying to act a damn fool. Really? I don't think you want to do that," I said with clinched teeth.

She said that she was tired of pretending that I meant nothing to her and her nothing to me. That she was more to me than just a fuck. Pushing me on the bed, she began to unzip my pants pulling me out. Before I knew it, she had me in her mouth doing what she did best. Damn, I couldn't move even if I wanted to. I felt like that 13-year-old kid enjoying myself, but praying not to get caught. The tricks she plays with that tongue ring is not a joke. It didn't take long before I came. I think it was a combination of her and the fact that Dani could come looking for me. She swallowed as she always did.

"I know she is not doing you like this. I can see it all on your face." She said as she wiped my excess from the corner of her mouth.

I jumped up and zipped my pants up. "Damn girl, you can't keep doing shit like this. I told you that I am in love with Dani."

"Fuck Dani," she said as she walked out the room.

I zipped up my pants, peeked out the door, and went back downstairs. I felt fucked that I allowed myself to be vulnerable. My life could have been gone for a nut. I should be more careful.

As far as Candy, there has to be a way to pull me from her gravitational pull. Sexually, I can't deny her. She pleases me. I don't love her. I love

Dani! I can't wait until I graduate so that I can spend the rest of my life with the woman I love.

Wes

I got in where I fit. I wasn't an original, but I am here to stay. A lot of times you fall in love with the thought of being in love and other times it just happens. Me, it just happened, and I will fight to keep it. Just hadn't decided if and when it will be necessary. Call me what you want; an escort, a trick, a bottom bitch, or even a manwhore; but just know you can call me satisfied when I am with her.

Wes

Like clockwork, every second Friday of the mouth The Men of Exquisite represents deep at The Gentlemen's Club. Bottles poppin' and ass shakin'. As usual, Rick is stuck in the corner getting his bimonthly lap dance. That dude is comical. Music so loud you can barely hear your heartbeat. Half off the top shelf brought them in droves. I am a Corona and lime man myself. Most females that frequent are either dancers, women who accompany their men expecting sex later, and women who liked women. I always like to look around just in case I see something that I like. Shit, a niggah like me might get chosen. I looked down near the end of the bar and there she stood. Standing out amongst the others she had a glow about herself. She was familiar with the others, but I never laid eyes on her before tonight. She held mini conversations with some, spoke and nodded to the others. She was different for some reason. I could tell she was not a regular. At least not on Fridays.

She sat at the bar nursing her drink for about 20 mins. Sink or swim! I walked over to introduce myself.

"Excuse me; is anyone sitting next to you?" I said.

"No." She said and turned back facing forward.

"Thanks, My name is Wes, what's yours?"

"Dani! Nice to meet you," as she extended her hand.

I not only received it, I bought it to my lips and kissed the back. I can tell by her expression that she was either not used to this or wondering what the fuck was on my mind. Now it is time for me to spit game.

"Can I freshen your drink for you? Bartender, can you give the lady another one of what she is having?"

"Thank you!" she said, cracking a little smile.

"So, what brings you to The Gentlemen's Club?"

"Business"

"Business?!" I said with a perplexed look on my face. "What type of business?"

"Are you used to asking a woman so many questions when you first meet?"

"Well, if you want to get to know her, absolutely. No shame in my game."

"Good answer," she said

A minute passed. "Well, what type of business?" I asked breaking the silence.

"Before I get into all of that, you came over here asking me if anyone was sitting next to me knowing damn well there was not. I saw you looking at me from VIP. You waited for about, "looking at her watch, "20 mins to come over with that lame line."

"Damn, that was cold." My smile left slowly. Looking stoned-faced, she continued to read me my rights.

"Not for sure how often you frequent The Gentlemen's Club or any club for that fact, but let me give you the game. If you see a woman you like, and you get up the nerve to step, let her know you have been looking at her. Because depending on how big or small the place is, if you are worth your w,eight she probably already clocked you."

"So, you are saying you like what you see?" I said as I started to smile again.

"Obviously you haven't heard a word I said. But that is cool. Now I need for you to pay attention. Since you didn't know how to step to me. Let me step to you." She said sternly.

"I'm listening," I said a little taken back.

"I have a business proposition for you."

"That is?"

"I am in the beginning stages of starting my own escort business and I am looking for a few nice-looking brothers who are willing to go that extra mile?" She said rubbing her middle finger in my palm.

"So, you do think I am nice looking? I said again.

"Wow." She said and turned back around.

"Are you serious?" I said laughing.

"Am I smiling?"

The lights dimmed on the stage and then the beam of light crept from the left corner. Everyone knew what this meant. The show was about to start. The MC walked out. "Ladies and Gentlemen, welcome to The Gentlemen's Club! I am the owner and your MC for this evening. Tonight, for your viewing pleasure we will have ladies galore. Remember, no touching or your ass will be out of here. But before I get started, I want to introduce you to the love of my life outside of this club. Daddy's girl, my daughter, Dani!"

The spotlight flashed on us. She stood and waved her hand as if she was the queen of England.

The MC moved on with an intro. "Now she's sweet as can be. You want to lick her and stick her, and she won't melt. So, bring your dollars up and make it rain for Chocolate!"

Breaking our silence once again, "So Dani, you are Daddy's girl?"

"I am. Not trying to be funny, I don't have a lot of time for conversation that is not going any place. So, back to business, let me know if you would be interested in being my first. If not, I'll see you around." She said as she pushed her drink away to stand up.

"Hold up," I said as I grabbed her hand. "Your first what? Man?"

"I think with your looks, nice teeth, and your swag we can do some thangs. Well, outside of working on your pick-up line," she said with a smile.

Man, she was beautiful. Dani is a fantasy come true. Nice looking, sexy, and got game. She is propositioning me to get paid to sleep with women. "Okay, so let me get this straight. You want me to come and work for you going out with women and getting paid a steady check for I," I said

"Yeah!" she said

"Only on one condition, you give me the opportunity to be with you. I will even go one step further and find the other men for you. Deal"

"Deal," I said talking shit

We watched the rest of the show, exchanged phone numbers talked for about an hour and went to grab a bite to eat.

~~~~~

She kept her part of the bargain and I kept mine. I introduced her to four men from my group. Now it was time for me to do my job. She took me shopping. I didn't see anything wrong with the clothes I had but if she wanted to spend money on me, well, hey, I am all for it. We went to Golden Gate and shopped until I dropped. She bought me a couple Polo outfits, drawers included. What took the cake was having a tailored suit. I was thumbtack sharp.

She was bold and I liked it. Told me that I was sexy as fuck and that she wanted some dick. It threw me for a minute. I'm used to asking for pussy, but this new world is something nice and refreshing. So, when she told me to meet her out the way I knew what it was. She was intriguing. I was interested to know how she was in the bed. It's not good to talk shit to a female that you really want only to either not get it up or cum to fast. My cousin told me years ago and it has proven to work that before you have sex jack off to get that first nut out. This will make you last longer on the second nut.

We met at a spot off 90. I was not for sure how this was going to go down. Shit, I am used to pulling hoes, not being pulled. I felt a little nervous, but shit, I had to it together. This was my new job and I had to grab my nuts and act like a damn man. I knew one damn thing; I better stand up in it, show her what I am working with. I guess that night was my test to assure I keep my job. It would be fucked to get fired before I got started.

We started off okay. We discussed my duties with these other women. At the close of business, I began to undress allowing her to see me. Yeah, you can see biceps and depending on my shirt you can see I have a six-pack, but without shorts what you can't see is my well-toned legs and calf muscles. When I got buckin' naked the look on her face was priceless. In no time flat, she was undressed and ready. Cum hard or go home.

She lay there glowing as she did when she walked into the club. I rubbed up and down her thighs slowly, allowing her to feel my touch. Opening her legs, I began licking her slowly watching her hips twist. Seeing her reaction, I began to suck on her pussy's tongue, biting and sucking her flavor. I ate her for at least an hour, finger-fucking her until she called my name. Got her! I am sure she didn't see me coming. She started closing her thighs on my head. It was time for her to cum.

"Cum for me," I began talking her through it.

"I'm on my way. Bring me to you," she said hot and heavily.

She twitched for a while. Gripping my head for dear life. She CAME for me!

Practicing safe sex as always, I strapped up before I got it in. I began kissing her from her nape to her belly button. Since I had already been down below, I headed back up stopping at her firm breast. I began sucking and licking her nipples; my dick throbbed, anticipating her warmth. I rubbed my head up and down, teasing her so that she would beg for this dick. She flinched, and her pussy opened for entry. She took me in. I fucked the shit out of her, evident in her face, sweat, and the fact she's going to have to get her hair done. Smiling to myself, I knew I had a keeper.

We started spending a lot of time together. It was nice and strange. Most women you fuck with aren't receptive to you fucking other women. I had the best of both worlds. Well, it would be nice if it lasted. All the time we were together, I had no idea that she had a man. He was away at college and was due to visit this summer. My heart was broken when she first told me. His name is Al and they had been friends since they were around 13/14 and been a couple ever since. He started visiting his aunt and the rest is history. Since she doesn't have a problem with me sleeping with other women, I guess I shouldn't mind her having a man. If I can keep her in my arms, I'm cool.

~~~~~

Up until now, Al has been just a phone call and text here and there. But the shit got real when she left to go and pick him up from the airport. It was summer and his time to visit. If I want her I should comply with the rules of the game. I knew he existed, but he was never an issue until now. Damn! I guess I can't be mad because I go out on dates, make money, and fuck some beautiful women and some not so good lookin'. Then I go home (well to her home) and get in bed and cuddle, breathe and relax. Lying in her arms at night after wooing and possibly fucking is the highlight of my existence. I'm in love. I would have never thought to see myself like this 8 months ago.

We all gathered at Dave's for his homecoming. I can't imagine what the big deal is. Why a surprise party? Shit, from what I am told he comes every year. When they walked in, everyone yelled "Welcome home. I stood there trying to mask my feelings. Happy, I was not. I stood there and watched as they walked around arm and arm greeting and chatting with everyone. I can't stand it. Trying to look like the happy couple. Shit, little does he know we are the happy couple. He is just a visitor. I keep her bed warm at night. I stay in between her legs. I'm the one that dicks her down, eats her pussy! And he is the one that is getting the praise.

I texted her, "This some bullshit! I don't know what the big deal is? But I am out of here. Can I see you upstairs for a minute before I bounce? Come to your Dad's office."

She responded, stating she would be there shortly. I mingled for a while and excused myself. Walking up the stairs glancing back towards the crowd. I went into the office, careful that no one to see me and waited. I think I have displayed and expressed myself repeatedly how I felt about her. I have given her all of me. She made money from me, I gave her money, and most importantly, I gave her my love.

I got instantly hard when she walked in the room. Closing and locking the door, I pushed her down on the couch, lifting her skirt, pulling her panties over I began to suck and bite. Knowing that her man was downstairs and anyone at any time could know what I was doing made this exciting and hot. So, I dove in, resisting her struggle. She wanted me to stop, evident by her pushing me away with a force which shortly subsided with her light moans. I licked her up and down quickly stopping long enough to suck on her sweet clit. Knowing how she likes for me to eat with my hands, I stuck my fingers in, listening to her body language. Screaming silently as she twerked her hips and seductively danced to my tune, I became lost in her moment. Having studied her motions. Calculating when she will burst, releasing her nectar ,I wanted to join in as her partner slow dancing to our music. I unbutton my pants, releasing myself snatching her up flipping her over the back of the couch, grabbing her arm, twisting it around her back she was under arrest. I stuck my dick in with force, assaulting her pussy. Banging, I reached in front, cupping her fat juiciness as a part of my search and seizure until she buried her face, muffling her scream of pleasure. Not for sure how long we were at it, time escaping, I tensed up knowing that I was cumming. I let her arm go and put my head on her, backbiting gently to mask my arrival. I CAME!

She wasn't there yet. With my body tuned to hers, my dick was still hard enough to continue her pleasure. It took a few more pumps and voila! She shook in pleasure as I held on to her every move.

We exit cautiously assuring that we were not caught. I hurried to the bathroom where I cleaned myself up. I splashed water on my face in the realization of what just transpired, I returned to the party. Knowing what I just did (or what I just got away with), I walked downstairs with a smile on my face. At this moment, I ain't trippin'. This niggah will be long gone, and I will be back in her bed real soon.

Candy

I'm all over the place. That could be a good thing. It is a struggle being me, but at the same time, I always land on my feet.

Candy

I love sex! Period point blank. It took me a long time to get to this point because for a while it was a chore. I was raped as a young girl and my mother was so wasted that I don't think she heard me when I told her. Because in my heart of hearts, I think if she did hear me she would have done something about it. She was promiscuous. She loved men. So, I had many uncles in my life, but not one dad.

I longed for a long time to have that dad that looked out for me. To tell me that it was okay. To fuck that niggah up for putting his hands on me. The one that had talks with you and tells you right from wrong. He didn't have to be rich. He just had to be there. I would have even taken a dad that was semi-there with an addiction. He couldn't be high all the time. (Or could he?) Just a percentage of what I didn't have in a male role model or figure would be cool with me. I knew he was not dead because she received money from him every month.

When he first took my innocence from me, I thought I was going to die. The pain of it all was just unbearable. I am not just talking about the sex. I am talking about the emotional toll it took over me. I felt dirty for a long time. Like I said, my mother was not a mother. She just made sure I had the bare minimum. The rest went to her addiction. I got tired of being teased at school for having a crack-headed mother and less than what my peers had. One day after talking to my counselor at school who I want to thank for introducing me to that side of me that could make a true difference in the world, she taught me that if I studied, I could get good grades. With good grades came scholarships and money. Now I had to dress the part. With no extra money in the house I had to fake it until I can make it.

My mother knew when the crave was real, she would sell just about anything. She was a functioning crackhead. So, we had good days. We had a decent place to stay, thanks to my father. From what I was told, he owned several houses and had several children. He didn't want us to live in the PJs. Can't say the lights were on all the time, but I never starved. I had locks on my bedroom door so not only didn't my shit come up missing, but I didn't have any unwanted visitors creeping. I had a mini apartment of my own. I had a microwave, mini-fridge, and a TV alongside my bed. I tried to make it as comfortable as possible despite what went on the other side of my door. One day while blocking out the obvious party in the other room there was a rerun of the Cosby show. Oh, how I loved the Cosby vibe. The TV show is what I would love for my life to be like. Mother, father, brother, and sisters. Anyway, this episode was when Denise tried to make some money and offered to make Theo a replica of a Gordon Gartrell. Denise fucked that shirt up. It sparked something in me. I went to some of the local stores and begged for some jobs. With no luck for over a month, I decided to offer to volunteer at the local seamstress shop for the leftover scraps after I cleaned up. Although she thought hard, she couldn't beat the free labor, cleanup, and disposal. And that is how it began. I watched and learned. Became a decent seamstress. Especially when I returned to school after summer break. The teasing stopped. I dressed better then all them hoes.

With my new look, I tried to hang out with the big girls. And the place to be was The Gentleman's Club. I was not old enough to go in, so I hung outside. I met this nice lady who frequents the club. I think she was a dancer, but I wasn't for sure. Every chance I got I would approach her and ask her what did I have to do to get in and a part of the scene. She told me that this was not a place for me. But what she would do is give me a couple dollars to make her a few outfits. So that is how our friendship began.

Most of the time she would try to get me to leave. Said this really wasn't a place for me. She gave me that education speech that I was used to receiving from someone who thought my life could be so much better than it was. For some reason, Stace didn't seem like the other ladies that I saw go in and out the club. She had something different or special about her. I guess you can say she was not ghetto -mouthed.

She mentioned that there was a night where kids my age would come to the club and enjoy themselves. My times just hanging out began to dwindle, and I started to only go on those nights. I think she was pleased that I chose a different path. One day while dropping off an outfit I made for her, she asked if I was interested in making some additional money. Hell yeah, I was. She needed a babysitter from time to time. She said she couldn't pay that much, but from where I was standing, an beats nan. In a matter of a year, I went from ashy to classy.

Stace called me one evening to come and babysit her son Al for a few hours. I figured babysitting for a thirteen -year-old wouldn't be hard. He would be fed by the time I got there and ready for bed. I would just watch TV, chill, and get paid. I arrived on time and settled on the couch to watch TV. It wasn't my first time at her house, so I was comfortable. Al came out of the back room and I couldn't believe my eyes. Maybe I hadn't looked at his pictures clearly, but this thirteen-year-old boy didn't look so thirteen. He had a body that wouldn't wait. At least not for me. My impure thoughts started rolling around in my head. I should be a damn shamed of myself that I felt the need to seduce this little boy.

Shortly after Stace left I walked past Al's room to see him undressing. What the fuck? For him to be a young boy he had a dick on him. Being naturally horny I had to see what that was all about. I am sure he doesn't know what to do with all he has. I need to be the first to let him tap that. I called him into the living room. I was naked with my legs gapped. My first thought was I hope that he knows what to do. As he approached sheepishly, I knew then that he was a virgin. I had worked myself up that there was no way to back down, not to mention that I am lying here naked on his mother's couch with my legs spread eagle like no one's business. He hesitated, looking scared but excited at the same time. If I didn't see it on his face, I sure could tell that his dick was moving outward, which made me even wetter than I had already made myself by playing. I told him I had a secret to tell him and he couldn't tell anyone what I had to say or show him.

I watched him as he approached me slowly. I can tell he has never seen anything as sexy and tasty as I was right then. In arms reach I grabbed his hand and helped him to feel on my C cups. Nice, firm and ripped as a summer melon. The closer he got to me, put him in my personal space. If I felt violated, I could defend myself. Since I invited him into my circle, I decided to take charge of my destiny. I grabbed him by his collar and helped him to the floor where on his knees, he was close enough where I could stick my tongue in his mouth. Clearly, he didn't know how to French kiss, but he would learn that day. It didn't take that long for him to catch on. This made me hotter than ever. I put his hand on my pussy to feel my wetness. I only had to tell him one time to lick and suck on my titties. Damn, I want something in me to put this fire out. I planned on playing with myself when he went to sleep anyway, so I came prepared and bought my mini toy bag. I gave him something to play with. In the right position, I can get down and maybe bust a nut or two. But if you can get someone else to do it for you, it can be orgasmic. I handed him my pink Vibetastic and told him what to do. He followed directions wonderfully. I wasn't for sure if he knew what he was doing or not, but he was hitting all the right spots. My body took over a little and did a little dance of its own. I felt him looking at me as he inched his way down to look directly at my pussy.

"Lick it." I moaned.

"Lick what?" he said.

I explained to him as quickly as I could in between moans of my anatomy. The clit and the hole. Where I wanted his attention. Where I wanted him to lick first and then second still maintaining the flow of my vibe. Damn, it felt so good. It didn't take me long to bust. I grabbed his head and held on for dear life while I drowned him in my juices.

I summoned him on top. He took out my toy and replaced it with him. When I tell you, this boy was holding, he was holding. For his age, I think he was at least 8 inches and thick. So nwt it was time to instruct him how I liked to be fucked. In and out. Up and down. Side to side. After a while, he picked up his own groove. I guess it was starting to feel good to him. He had a few choice words that I did not have a problem with. I whispered in his ear and held on to his small but tight ass and talked him into his nut. It didn't take him long after that to cum. He rolled off me and sat on the couch with his eyes closed.

I wasn't finished. He didn't know that until I stuck his dick in my mouth. Now most men when they dick goes soft it shrivels. If that was the case for him, he didn't go far. His dick was still long enough for me to do something with. It began to grow and when it was fully hard, I went to town. I think his dick touched every side of my mouth. Right jaw, left jaw, roof, and under my tongue and I rotated it around his beautiful dick. After I had him where I wanted, it was time to take him to the moon and back. I pushed it in and sucked it until it reached my tonsils. He cried out. He grabbed my head and pushed it down more. I guess he liked it and wanted more. So, I gave him more until he came.

It seemed like as soon as he came I heard Stace's car door closed. We jumped up. He ran to the bathroom and I attempted to straighten up as much as possible, throwing on my clothes and spraying the room with air freshener to get rid of the sex smell that I knew was in the air. When she cleared the door, he walked out the bathroom rubbing his eyes as if he woke up to go to the bathroom. I don't think Stace was wise to the fact that I just fucked her son. Her thirteen-year-old son. The dick was soooo good that every chance I got to get some of that, it was on and poppin'.

~~~~

As the years passed, I was a regular in Al's bed. We had no commitment because he said he was promised to another. Maybe I should have approached him sooner with the proposition. I am not for sure how serious he is with her because we share our bodies with one another as often as possible. It wasn't unheard of for me to catch a flight to see him. His parents were kind of strict, from what he says. So, going to his house was a no-no. That was fine. I was old enough to rent a room. So that is what I did.

The older he got, the more he stood up in it. I don't know if he had been practicing with someone or not, but when I tell you it felt like he was working through some problems and I was the one he took everything out on: It felt good. The only thing was, when it was over, it was over, and I began to feel some type of way. I started to wonder how those who have sex on a regular can take the feelings out of it. Sex to me is emotion and mine are starting to run deep for Al. I understand that there is at least a five-year gap between us, but he is undeniably dreamy. I think I love him.

~~~~

I started taking a few classes at the local Community College. I became a great seamstress and wanted to step up my game. It was time to start making real money. The only thing is I didn't have much to invest. I had to have a talk with my mom about who my father was. Hopefully, she could tell me, and I can show him how I turned out and what my plan is and maybe, just maybe, he would invest. If not, it was time to get my inspector gadget on. Dig deep for clues. I am sure she has something around the house that will reveal his identity.

~~~~

Cindy was a functional crackhead, so every day wasn't always so bad. I explained to her my dream and wanting to open my own shop. She was happy about the idea. Not for sure if it was because of me fulfilling a dream or the fact that there would be potential money coming into the house. Whatever the case was, I was glad that she was listening and willing to support. This was my chance to crack on who my dad was. And of course, as always, she didn't want to reveal. So, I was okay with that for the time being. I didn't need any more distractions. My plate was full. I had a second-hand sewing machine that I purchased from Mrs. Winters at the shop I was working. I had multiple orders from the ladies at The Gentlemen's Club, and slowly but surely some of the girls from school reached out for some of my creations.

~~~~

Stace was telling me about someone she knew who was going to school for business and that she was opening her own. I asked if she would introduce, so I could pick their brain. She did. Her name was Dani. She was a cute girl. Naturally long curly hair. Nice body. I thought she was a dancer at The Gentlemen's Club because that is where we met over drinks. She gave me some directions and info to follow up on. I was grateful for what she gave. As I sat there soaking up the music and enjoying the atmosphere I overheard Dani and Stace talking about Al. My ears perked and I was no longer vibing to the tunes, but ear hustling to what they were saying about my man. Wasn't much info, but what she had planned for him when he came in from school. Some type of surprise party. You know I was all ears at this point. But really fucked me up was to find out that Mister was her dad. This bitch had money.

~~~~

I would see Dani around from time to time boo'd up with this Wes. Wes would frequent the club with his boys on certain days. I tried to holla at him one day and he told me that he was spoken for. Shit, I guess he is. Let me get this right, Al and Dani and Wes. I wonder if Al knows about

Wes. Probably not. Dani doesn't know about me. I wonder if I should tell him about his Miss Perfect.

~~~~

I went to visit Al for a quick fix. I love our time together. Except for when his precious Dani calls. Whatever we are doing, when that number flashes, he shut shit down. I must sit there and not say anything. Stay in my lane. Do I like that shit? Hell nawl. But if I want to keep getting dicked down I must comply with his rules. Things are pretty much the same except he wraps up now to assure I don't get pregnant. How would he ever explain that to Stace let alone Dani?   I often tell myself I need to leave this dysfunctional relationship. But it is something about the dick and his touch that keeps me longing for more.

Summertime is here again. And as always, he is on his way to Dani for his yearly visit. He did mention that when school was over he was moving to be with her daily. I wasn't for sure how to feel about that at first, but as I thought about it, it puts him close to me. I don't have to fly across the world to see him. Between his house and college, I know I have accumulated some frequent flyer miles. His flight left at 6:55 pm so at 2:00 he climbed out of bed after giving me yet another blissful night/day of sex. I wanted to beg him so bad to stay, but I knew he would never miss a flight to see Dani. So, there I was left in bed with a wet ass while he ran a few errands before he left to see her.

I called the airline to see if I could get a soon flight out. It was just my luck that there was. I am sure he will be surprised to see me in town when he reaches there. I know I am walking on thin ice, but I just can't get enough of him. I just want more time. Will it be beneficial to let him know that his precious Dani is fucking that fine-ass niggah Wes? People think he just works for us. But I know better than that. You can see how that niggah look at her when they are around. Reminds me of what I think I look like when I'm around Al. As bad as I want to tell him about them it might backfire, and he might stop fucking with me. So, it is a true catch 22. Damn, iedf I do and damned if I don't. What the fuck is all this about?

~~~~

I called Stace to pick me up at the rapid station. This way she has no idea that I took a flight. Let alone a flight to fuck her nephew. She told me that they were having a surprise party for Al over at Dave's house.

"Wow, a surprise party? That is nice. What's the occasion?" I said.

"We want him to know that we are very proud of him for his accomplishments, and his grades are doing the damn thang." She said.

"This must be special if you are having it at Dave's house and not the club. I thought all parties were held at the club." I said.

"It was Dani's idea to have it at the house," she said proudly.

I just can't escape that damn name. Dani is perfect. Dani is this and Dani is that. Fuck Dani! "Okay, this should be nice then," I said with a hint of sarcasm in my voice. Couldn't let on to my displeasure of hearing her name.

When we got there everything was set up. I mean she went all out for this one. Steak and lobster dinner, humidors full of cigars, and bottles of Cristal just to name some of the things there. This was my first time at Dave's house. Rumors were bouncing around about how grand his house was. It looked like a mansion to me. It had at least six bedrooms and no telling how many bathrooms. Shit, my project could fit in one corner of this house. A bitch will soak this up. Take a few selfies and post on social media. #Flossing!

"Here they come!" someone yelled.

Everyone got quiet as the door knob turned. As soon as he walked in everyone yelled "Surprise!" Well, everyone but me. When he saw me, his eyes popped. Looked just like a deer in headlights. I raised my glass in the air to toast him. Not to his surprise, but for yet another awesome fuck. I scanned the room and saw Wes standing on the sideline with a sour ass face. This niggah salty as fuck. His bitch's man is in town and he have to wait until it's his turn. Stay in his lane like I have to stay in mine. Dani's boys were all huddled in a corner together talking and sipping. Wes kept texting and looking at his phone. The uneasiness on his face said it all. But I am sure I am the only one that peeped it. Because everyone else was enjoying themselves getting drunk off $300-

plus bottles of wine. At some point, I watched Dani look at her phone a couple times. Oh shit, he is texting her and she is texting him. These motherfuckas are bold as fuck.

She excused herself and walked away. I looked around and didn't see Wes. His ass left. Wow. I guess he is salty as fuck. Still surveying the room, I noticed that Al was getting tired of all the chit-chat. He excused himself. He must be going to look for his precious Dani. I need a diversion. I need to talk to him. Not for sure if I am going to tell him about Dani and Wes. I just know I need to say something. I walked around and slid upstairs to look around. As soon as I saw Al hit the top of the stairs I walked down and grabbed him by the arm and asked for a word.

"I'm busy right now. I will talk to you later, he said, rather aggravated.

"It will not take that long. Just give me a few seconds of your time. Please," I pleaded.

"I'm looking for Dani; have you seen her?" He said.

"No, I wasn't looking," I said rather heatedly.

"I have no clue why you are tripping. We had this conversation already. I told you. Why are you here anyway? Didn't I leave you back on campus?" he said as he pulled me into the guest bedroom to continue the conversation.

"I love you," she said.

"Okay, I got it. But why are you telling me this right now? Today is not the day for all this. Dani is here, somewhere in this house. She can walk up at any moment and you are trying to act a damn fool. Really? I don't think you want to do that." He said with clenched teeth.

"I am tired of pretending that you mean nothing to me and I mean nothing to you. I am more than just a fuck. I have been in a relationship with you for just as long as you have known her, I said. I pushed him to the bed, pulled his dick out, and sucked it up in one fell swoop. I wasn't for sure if he was startled, shocked, or scared of getting caught. I rolled my tongue, letting him feel my tongue ring. He likes that. It does something to him. If I hit the right spot a couple times, he will come in no time. Not to mention he loves when I swallow.

I licked my lips to make sure I caught everything. Wiping the corners of my mouth to double check there was no evidence. He was so sweet.

Al jumped up and zipped his pants. "Damn, girl, you can't keep doing this shit. I told you that I am in love with Dani."

"I know she is not doing you like this. If she was, you wouldn't keep coming to me," I said cockily. "I can see it all over your face when that orgasm hits you. So, fuck Dani, I said as I walked out the room.

Dave

I am the glue to it all. Everything touches me at some point in time, even if I wasn't aware of it. They call me Mister and for good reason.

Dave

My life was not always silky. I went without many a nights. That is why I promised myself when I grew up and had children, that there would never be a reason to go hungry. Times were hard, and I truly understood that my mother did the best that she could. But her best was not enough all the time. My father was MIA. I didn't fault him not being with my mother. What I didn't like is that he wasn't with me. Again, another promise to myself, if I was to have any children that they will not go without even if I wasn't with their mothers.

I have a total of twelve biological children and five or six wanting to be. That is cool. They are welcomed. Most likely they were my children's siblings. Let us see: there are David Jr., Doug, Rob, Sheila, Marsha, Queen, Marcus, Candace, Darnell, and Danielle. As I said, my children will never be without if I had anything to do with it. Never wanted to be in the system. So, I gave my children's mothers a monthly stipend. Out of all those babies' Mamas, I was only married to one of them. Her name was Danielle. I loved her so much that when she finally had a baby, I had to name her after her. I would have had more children, but she kept miscarrying. Not for sure why this was happening to us, and it made her sad all the time. When she had Dani, it became her project.

I didn't have true relationships with the other women. For real, I haven't seen most of my children since they were babies. That didn't stop me from supporting them. I was married to Danielle and although I owned The Gentlemen's Club and had a few women, she was okay with that. I knew the rules of my house and I obeyed them. A pimp being pimped. My women knew what it was, and they respected the game.

Big Dani was the business mind behind most of all my ventures. Most were her ideas to begin with. I had the capital and from there we were ballers in a sense. I owned a few houses and the club. At first, I was going to buy houses for all my children's mothers, but we decided against it. They wouldn't pay rent and still think I am supporting the children. Which is my duty as a parent to take care of my kids, but to house them and their niggahs was not a part of the deal. So every month like clockwork, they all received a stipend. Some of my children visited from time to time, most with their hands out and others just came to visit. So

I guess, thinking about it, it is sad to say that I can walk past one of my children and don't know who they are. But guess who I did know? My baby girl, Dani.

When Dani was ten years old her mother became ill. It rocked everyone. She forged on until she became too weak to continue her daily tasks. She never let on that she was not feeling well. She made sure baby girl was okay. They spent a lot of time together in that bedroom talking about who knows what. As her time neared, Dani never left her side. I could feel the cloud over our house. She made me continue to go to work so that I continue to handle my business and assure that I could take care of my children, even though most of them were grown and had kids on their own. Of all my ladies, the only way that she was partial to was Stace. When she was unable to keep the house, she requested her to come and assist with Dani.

She fought a good fight.

~~~~

Dani was devastated. I had to step up and be what she needed. Have her front when she needed me and her back for when she needed to be held up. I think I was a little harsh or brutal with my delivery, but I am sure she knew that I was coming from a good place. I told her about life from a man's perspective. I am a man and can't really raise a girl child, but I can tell her the things I know from her mother and from dealing with my other women daily. I think we had the "talk" early. I held no bars from her. She couldn't say she didn't have the tools to survive. We talked about her period and how she was to handle her hygiene. Boys most definitely was a topic, because I was one before. Most importantly, how to take care of yourself financially and not to depend on anyone outside of myself. I think she took me to my word. Life lessons of an alpha male to his baby girl.

~~~~

I watched her closely. She did well in school. I saw her when she fell in love. I was kind of hesitant about it at first. His name was Al and he was Stace's son. And for years I saw them inseparable. He appeared to be nice for her. So, I let them be. As she got older I saw a change in my baby girl. She was becoming a woman. And with that came sex. I don't think she knows that I know she lost her virginity. It was written all over her face. But if that was the secret she thought to keep, then her secret it is.

~~~~

I am an old man with a shitload of swag. I am that old pimp-ass niggah with the fly clothes. No, I am not in a time warp. I dressed to the nines. Won't see me with fifty-million gaudy rings on my fingers and a fat gold chain hanging from my neck with my shirt open trying to entice the ladies. I am that niggah. With some hair dye, you wouldn't tell I was in my late sixties. My wife taught me consistency and my word is my bond. My actions bring me reactions and I always handle my business, whatever it was at the time. The club was my baby outside of Dani. I was there every day.

I taught her about my business and how to manage my properties. I knew that I wasn't going to be here forever, and I needed to know that all my hard work wasn't for nothing. Although I had sons, and one would think you would pass your legacy down to them, but they were more mama's boys than anything. So, Dani was mine and I took her up under my wing. She was my successor. She was my mini-me.

I started to slow down despite what I thought I wanted to do. Dani noticed and sacrificed going away to school. She said it was her duty to take care of me as I have taken care of her her entire life. I wanted to argue with her, to make her go away to school, but she wouldn't have it. So, there we were the dynamic duo, Frick and Frack, the wonder twins.

I was so happy when she proposed to me handling men as I did women. Well, it was a little different. Her escort service sounded wonderful. She showed me her plans along with a financial statement that made me want to cry it was so good. I gave her my blessings. With that, she became a Mademoiselle. She had roughly five, I think. I hadn't had the opportunity to meet them all. Heard she was hanging tight with one particular person. His name is Wes. I heard nothing but good things about him. Without being in her business, I had to see if she was serious. Put your money where your mouth is. I deliberately removed Al from the picture for a minute to see how she was going to handle things. She was caught up in her new world that it seemed like Al was a thing of the past. So, when she came to me and told me that she had developed feelings for Wes I was not shocked. However, I had to come clean and tell her what I did. She was a little peed, but she will get over it.

~~~~

The days leading up to her surprise party for Al, I was not feeling the best. I had to wear the face that showed differently. Couldn't worry her when she was handling so much. Not to mention I was so curious to see how she was going to play her hand with Wes and Al in the same room together. Oh, how exciting. Of course, I never said anything to Stace, seeing as though that is her son. Dani hid her relationship with Wes well. So, I guess my baby has secrets of her own and who am I to bust them out. She will tell when she wants to share.

She went all out for this party. Lobster, Cristal, and Cigars named a few things that were there. The party was rather expensive, if you ask me. But if that is what she wants, then that is what she gets. I was just waiting to see how things turned out.

I was a little winded, but you couldn't keep me home. You couldn't pay me to miss someone's face when it hit the fan that Dani was me. Holding it down for her Pops. Everyone was there and eagerly waiting for Al and Dani to arrive. We sat around and mingled. Everyone knew each other except for a few I didn't recognize. I am sure at some point I will find out who these strangers were in my house. But for now, I must be the perfect host.

Stace came in with a young lady that I saw frequent the club from time to time. No clue who she was; I guess I will learn who she is as well. About five minutes later, someone yelled that they were coming. We all took our places and waited for them to open the door.

"Surprise!" everyone yelled.

Al looked shocked. He was happy to see everyone, but sort of perplexed as to why they were there for him. Dani explained how proud she was of him and his accomplishments that she wanted to show him just how much. Everyone began to mingle. At some point, Dani decided to introduce me to her gentlemen. I shook all their hands and formally introduced myself. Shortly after, all the chit-chat amongst folks, I noticed Al and Dani were missing. If my memory serves me correctly, so is Wes and the one lady that came with Stace. I guess folks want to have some privacy. Let the kids be kids is what I have said in the past.

~~~~

My health is failing. I thought I could continue my front. I should sit down with Dani and give her my directives just in case something happens sooner than later. I called my lawyer to set up my will and other transfers. I had to make sure that my wishes were carried out, and the right person for that was Dani. My true ride-or-die chick. Since her mother is not here to instruct me on how I should handle everything, I got the next best thing. I have ten biologicals plus the other five. I have to make sure they are taken care of. Dani and I put together a list of all my assets and all the children. Everyone was grown and had their own lives to live. I remember at one point or another I had a visit from the majority of all my children. But as time went on, I saw less and less of them. Especially when the child support ended.

Dani

Well, by this time you have learned about my family and friends. I wouldn't trade them for the world. I say my life is together even if a change of events occurred that will knock some folks down. I am a woman raised by an alpha male.

Dani

The inevitable happened. I can't say I didn't see it coming. For that last few months, we decided to prepare for this day. But are you truly ready? I wasn't. The night before, Daddy wanted to go over to the house and sit and talk to Mama. I didn't find it to be strange because he has conversations with her all the time. I just think he felt closer to her when he was at our old house. I packed an overnight bag and joined him. He never changed anything about the house. I guess that is how he liked it. Called it the simpler times. Well anyway, times were not going to be simpler for me. This is when life begins.

~~~~

When I found him, I thought he was sleeping peacefully. He laid there as if he was cuddled with someone. I believe that he spent one last night with my mother before he transitioned. I sat at the edge of the bed and cried uncontrollably for about 20 mins before I realized I needed to get up and go. There were things that I needed to do and people I needed to call. Couldn't figure out who to call first. Do I call Stace, Al, Wes or the police/EMS/Corner? Shit, shit, shit! It has been a long time shit I didn't feel in control. I took a deep breath, got up off the bed, kissed him, and left the room to retrieve my phone. I sat at the kitchen table and called Stace first. That was truly a difficult call. I know that she loved my dad dearly. After I hung up from her I called Al, Wes and then 911 in that order. Stace made it there before the police and EMS. The town was small so I know it would not take long before the news would spread.

Al wanted to take a flight, but I assured him that he could come when I made the arrangements. There was no need for him to miss school. What he didn't know is that I had Wes to be by my side. I knew that everybody and their mama would be coming to the house. After the coroner's office took Daddy's body, I headed home to get ready for all these guests and to put things in motion for his funeral and the reading of the will.

People started coming in droves. It was expected. I had food for those who wanted to stay and eat. Which we know all of them did. People talked about Daddy positively. I was surprised that folks were bearing gifts. I received a gang of cards. There were women who claimed to be the mother of his children that I have never met and whose name was in the will. It is not like I can ask him if he ever laid with anyone of them. Mama's baby, Daddy's maybe. I knew of his lifestyle and the likelihood of him having more children is not impossible. I will have them do a DNA test and if they are his children I will assure that they receive something. For some reason in the back of my mind, I knew that there will be women who would come out of the woodwork.

~~~~

Daddy's service was packed. There was no parking at the funeral home. Shuttle buses were dropping people off. When the family car arrived, people were standing in line to go in. I entered the funeral home sugga sharp. I wore a black, wide-legged pantsuit, red shirt, and a black pair of Christian Louboutin red-bottom pumps. My hair was flawless. I was Queen. And today I was laying my King to rest. I was so glad that no one cut up. The way I was feeling, I would have had their asses escorted out. The mayor spoke along with other important people in the community. A few of his children's mothers told of their time together and how he was a wonderful man. I sat there in the front row with Al on my right and Wes on my left. I let Stace sit in the first seat. Although, my mother was his only wife, Stace was a perfectly fine substitute.

The procession line was blocks long. Police escorts not only headed and ended the procession line, but they blocked off streets. It was truly a homegoing celebration.

After we left the burial, everyone met at the reception hall attached to The Gentlemen's Club. I knew I would have to mingle, so I took my twenty-five-minute shoes off. I truly looked good with them on. But there is no way I could continue to walk in them all day. I changed into my flats. The hall was packed. It almost looked like a cabaret. Good food and good drink. I should have sold set-ups to make money for all these women who are claiming that they have children by Dave. The food was catered and we had plenty of it. I was approached by so many people that it is still a blur as to who actually showed. One thing that I do know, both Al and Wes were there. Wes was truly being a trooper. He had to play his position as he always did when Al was in town. But that did not negate his role and what he was to do for me. He just had to be careful as to how he did it.

~~~~

The house felt different the day after although I still felt his presence. There is no way I could deal at this point being home alone. Of course, with Al still in town, he was there. Unfortunately, he would have to return to school for finals. The reading of the will is in two days, so I had to prepare for that. Although I already know what is in it. I am almost scared to see how ratchet his baby-mamas are. Although their kids are grown, they will still be there with their hands out. My dad wasn't selfish, so I guess I can throw a dog a bone.

~~~~

I arrived at Salam, Taylor and Fisher law firm around 8:30 am. The reading is set to start at 9:30 am. I needed to breathe. I had to double check that I had my checkbook so I can disburse this money. Before I get out of this car, I should pray that everything runs smoothly and these people will not act a fool. But on a serious note, I don't know most of these people. I knew I had brothers and sisters, but not many came to visit throughout my childhood so of course, they were not around while I was growing up. For the ones that did, we had a pretty decent relationship. I guess the reading of the will could be classified as a reunion of some sorts. Woosah!

I must make a fashionably late entrance. I sat in my big body truck and watched as men and women as they entered the building. Some came out of cars and others were walking from the street. I guess they were on public transportation. I couldn't necessarily pinpoint who was who and if they were all there for the reading. I looked at my watch, it was 9:25 am. I had to make another grand entrance. This time I wore a blue flare dress and some blue and white houndstooth designed shoes. With of course the matching shoulder bag. These bitches can't see me, I thought to myself as I stepped off the elevator.

I surveyed the room for familiar faces. I saw a couple of my siblings that I remembered. Some faces I saw at the service. I nodded as I walked in to have a seat. Stace was sitting across the room so I headed her way because right then she was the comfort that I was looking for.

We were all called into the conference room where I took my place at the head of the table. The lawyer began reading the will.

"I, David C. Jones, am writing my last will and testament not to be mistaken for any others…" The lawyer said.

By the time he was finished my dad acknowledge all his children. As we agreed upon, he gave them each 10K. I wrote the checks out. But of course, I needed to see ID and birth certificates. Many didn't take too kindly to me asking them to validate if they were his children or not. I was trying to figure out what the fuck they thought. If I didn't know them, they could have walked off the damn street trying to take advantage. If they didn't have a birth certificate with his name on it. They had to have a DNA test right there. Fuck'em, he didn't work all those years just to give money away to strangers. Now my five siblings that were not his children, still got some money. One thing for certain and two things for sure: my Dad was not a bum-ass niggah, and if he had children by your mother, you were considered his.

After I passed out the checks, I noticed that there was still money to disburse but everyone picked up their check and left to the other room where we are going to hold the second part of the process. The first portion was the dispersing of monies to everyone who was receiving anything. The second portion was just for his children. I gave Stace a hug and told her that I will see her later. I believe she would be satisfied. He wanted her to live in one of his houses and gave her a car along with some money. I, of course, did not let everyone see what she received. I am sure holy hell would have broken out. At least the original children: DJ, Doug, Rob, Sheila, Marsha, Queen, Marcus, and Darnell showed. I met a few of them in passing. Some of them for the first time. We exchanged phone numbers and the promise to keep in touch. I had nieces and nephews that I have never met.

I sat perplexed as to why my sister Candace did not show up? Was she at the funeral? Maybe she didn't know that Daddy passed away.

As I was leaving out, the lawyer told me that my sister Candace was in route. That her car broke down and a tow truck recently arrived and is dropping her off at the office. I am sure this money would come in handy for her. I sat out in the lobby and waited for her arrival. The door opened and it was Candy.

"Hey, you, what are you doing here?" she said.

"I'm here waiting for my sister. Why are you here?" I questioned.

"Some family business," she said.

"Okay, I hope it is not too bad," I returned.

"Sorry to hear about Mister. He was a good man," she praised.

"He was, and I will miss him dearly. But you know me, I will maintain," I said.

"How is Al?" she asked.

"He is wonderful. Thanks for asking. Matter fact, he just left last night," I said.

She sat down next to me to continue are conversing.

She mentioned how she thought Wes was a cutie pie. I told her that I knew and that he was one of my gentlemen. I started to ask her if she was interested, but clearly, she was. I left that alone because I truly know I didn't know want her to have her hands on him. To change the subject, I asked her how her clothing business was coming alone. She said she was doing fine. I congratulated her on her success. She said thanks to my advice, she made some changes and upped her game. I told her I was glad that I could help.

Shortly after, the lawyer's secretary came out to call me back to the back. I got up and told Candy it was nice to see her again. And that I hoped things work out for her. She gave me back sentiments. Five minutes later the office door opens and Attorney Fisher said, "Danielle, this is your sister Candace. Candace, this is your sister Danielle." When I stood up and turned around and saw Candy, my heart skipped.

Candy

Dani is my sister. Does this mean I need to stop fucking my sister's man? Probably not, I wonder what Al will say when he finds out. Shit, he might turn away. This can be ever so twisted. I know I will continue to fuck him as long as he allows me. I know he enjoys himself when he is with me. The pussy is good and I know he is all in for my head game. I have been fucking him since he was thirteen, so the likelihood of him leaving will be slim. To see how strong his love for her is, will be interesting. Damn!